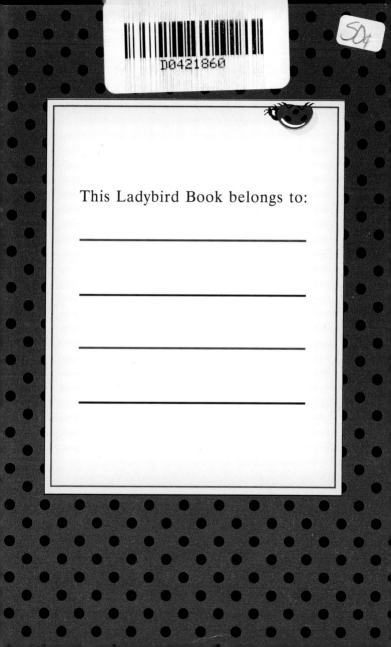

This Ladybird Book belongs to:

_____

_____

_____

_____

This Ladybird retelling
by
Ronne P Randall

Published by Ladybird Books Ltd
27 Wrights Lane London W8 5TZ
A Penguin Company
5 7 9 10 8 6 4

© LADYBIRD BOOKS LTD 1993

Printed in Italy

FAVOURITE TALES

Dick Whittington

illustrated
by
MARTIN AITCHISON

based on a traditional story

Many years ago there lived a boy called Dick Whittington.

Dick's mother and father had died when he was very young. There was

no one to look after him, and he was very poor, so he decided to go to London to seek his fortune.

He tied his belongings into a little bundle and set off down the road.

As soon as Dick got to London, he tried to find a job.

He went from street to street and from shop to shop, asking for work. But no one had a job to offer him.

When night fell, Dick was so tired and
weak from hunger that he sank down
on the nearest doorstep.

But a cook came out and angrily tried to chase Dick away. "Get off my master's doorstep, you lazy boy!" she shouted.

Just then, the master of the house came home. He was a rich merchant named Mr Fitzwarren, and he had a kind heart.

"Let the boy stay," he told the cook. "I'm sure you can find some work for him in the house."

So Dick was given a job in the kitchen and a room in the attic of the house.

Dick was busy during the day, but at night he felt sad and lonely. To make matters worse, dozens of rats and

mice ran through his room and across
his bed every night.

"If only I had a cat," Dick thought.
"She would be a friend to me, and she
would keep the rats and mice away."

Next day, Dick went to the market near the Tower of London. There he met a woman with a handsome cat to sell.

"She's very good at catching rats and mice," the woman said.

From then on, Dick was happier. He loved his cat, and every night she chased the rats and mice away from his bed.

"That's just what I need," said Dick. He bought the cat for a penny – all the money he had in the world.

Now Mr Fitzwarren owned many ships which sailed to distant lands with goods to sell. Whenever a ship sailed, Mr Fitzwarren let everyone in the house give the captain something to sell. That way, everyone could earn some extra money.

When it was time for the next ship to sail, Dick told Mr Fitzwarren he had nothing to send with the captain.

"Why don't you send your cat?" asked Alice, Mr Fitzwarren's daughter.

Dick did not want to lose his cat, but
he was fond of Alice and wanted to
please her. So he agreed.

Dick missed his cat, and soon the rats
and mice were tormenting him again.
He was so unhappy, he decided to run
away.

As Dick left London, he heard the
bells of Bow Church ringing. They
seemed to be singing,

"Turn again, Whittington,
Lord Mayor of London.
Turn again, Whittington,
Thrice Mayor of London."

"The bells are calling me back!"
thought Dick in amazement. Quickly,
he returned to Mr Fitzwarren's house.

Meanwhile, Mr Fitzwarren's ship had arrived in a far-off country. The King and Queen were holding a banquet in the captain's honour.

The servants carried in trays and platters of delicious food. But before anyone could take a bite, hundreds of rats swarmed into the room.

The captain knew just what to do. He rushed back to the ship and fetched Dick's cat.

The cat leapt out of his arms and went

straight for the rats. Those she didn't kill fled in terror.

"What a marvellous creature!" cried the King, who had never seen a cat. "If you will sell her to us, I will pay you handsomely."

When the ship returned to London, the captain had a chest of precious jewels for Dick.

"You are very rich now, Dick, my boy," said Mr Fitzwarren. "Your cat has made your fortune."

Dick could hardly believe his good
luck. Before he left Mr Fitzwarren's
house, he asked Alice to marry him,
and she joyfully agreed.

Dick and Alice lived happily together, and some years later, Dick became Lord Mayor of London. Indeed, he was Lord Mayor of London three times.

So the Bow Bells had been right when they had said to him,

*"Turn again, Whittington,
Lord Mayor of London.
Turn again, Whittington,
Thrice Mayor of London."*